S.W.I.T.C.H.
SERUM WHICH INSTIGATES TOTAL CELLULAR HIJACK

OXFORD
UNIVERSITY PRESS

Great Clarendon Street, Oxford OX2 6DP
Oxford University Press is a department of the University of Oxford.
It furthers the University's objective of excellence in research, scholarship,
and education by publishing worldwide in

Oxford   New York

Auckland   Cape Town   Dar es Salaam   Hong Kong   Karachi
Kuala Lumpur   Madrid   Melbourne   Mexico City   Nairobi
New Delhi   Shanghai   Taipei   Toronto

With offices in

Argentina   Austria   Brazil   Chile   Czech Republic   France   Greece
Guatemala   Hungary   Italy   Japan   Poland   Portugal   Singapore
South Korea   Switzerland   Thailand   Turkey   Ukraine   Vietnam

Oxford is a registered trade mark of Oxford University Press
in the UK and in certain other countries

British Library Cataloguing in Publication Data

Data available

ISBN: 978-0-9566276-1-2

1 3 5 7 9 10 8 6 4 2

Printed in Great Britain
Paper used in the production of this book is a natural,
recyclable product made from wood grown in sustainable forests
The manufacturing process conforms to the environmental
regulations of the country of origin

This book has been specially written and published for World Book Day 2011. World
Book Day is a worldwide celebration of books and reading, with events held last
year in countries as far apart as Afghanistan and Australia, Nigeria and Uruguay. For
further information please see **www.worldbookday.com**
World Book Day in the UK and Ireland is made possible by generous sponsorship
from National Book Tokens, participating publishers, authors and booksellers. Booksellers who accept the £1 World Book Day Token kindly agree to bear the full cost of
redeeming it

S.W.I.T.C.H.

SERUM WHICH INSTIGATES TOTAL CELLULAR HIJACK

Bug Battle

Ali Sparkes

illustrated by
Ross Collins

OXFORD
UNIVERSITY PRESS

DIARY ENTRY *562.4

SUBJECT: JOSH AND DANNY PHILLIPS

Huzzah! My Serum Which Instigates Total Cellular Hijack is a success! They don't call me, 'the greatest, most exceptional scientific genius EVER' for nothing, you know. Well, they don't call me, 'the greatest, most exceptional scientific genius EVER' at all. But one day they will!

I've already turned Josh and Danny from next-door into all kinds of creepy-crawlies with my extraordinary SWITCH spray. You would think they would have jumped at the chance to turn into a grasshopper, spider, fly or ant but all they do is moan! I admit nearly getting

REMEMBER →

$$\frac{4 \times \pi^2}{OS\text{-}7^*} \quad \sqrt{\frac{P_2}{0.8}} \times \frac{V_6^2 \, \text{o}/9}{9 \cdot 15\%} = \frac{4.198}{4.197} \quad \frac{60}{OUP} \to \not\!\!R \to \frac{1}{2} \text{st}$$

squished, eaten, and sizzled were small setbacks but honestly, they wouldn't appreciate a scientific break-through if it bit them on the bum!

I bet they'll stop complaining when I complete the REPTOSWITCH formula though. What boy wouldn't want to be turned into an alligator . . .

If only I could remember where I hid the crystal cubes containing the REPTOSWITCH formula. There'd be no stopping me if my arch enemy, Victor Crouch, hadn't wiped parts of my memory. I know he'll be watching me, trying to the get the formula before I do. Despite being the greatest, most exceptional scientific genius EVER, I still need those twins to help me find the missing cubes.

And when I do, Josh and Danny will be begging me to try out my REPTOSWITCH spray on them!

Bwah-ha ha ha ha ha aaaaaaahhhhhh!!!! urgh, a-hem, urgh . . . (Powerful, manic laughter . . . and yes, I know I ruined it a bit by choking on my Ovaltine but you get the general idea . . .)

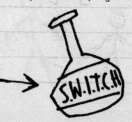

Danny and Josh
(and Piddle)

They might be twins but they're NOT the same! Josh loves insects, spiders, beetles and bugs. Danny can't stand them. Anything little with multiple legs freaks him out. So sharing a bedroom with Josh can be . . . erm . . . interesting. Mind you, they both love putting earwigs in big sister Jenny's pants drawer . . .

Danny
- FULL NAME: Danny Phillips
- AGE: 8 years
- HEIGHT: Taller than Josh
- FAVOURITE THING: Skateboarding
- WORST THING: Creepy-crawlies and tidying
- AMBITION: To be a stunt man

Josh

- **FULL NAME:** Josh Phillips
- **AGE:** 8 years
- **HEIGHT:** Taller than Danny
- **FAVOURITE THING:** Collecting insects
- **WORST THING:** Skateboarding
- **AMBITION:** To be an entomologist

Piddle

- **FULL NAME:** Piddle the dog Phillips
- **AGE:** 2 dog years
  (14 in human years)
- **HEIGHT:** Not very
- **FAVOURITE THING:** Chasing sticks
- **WORST THING:** Cats
- **AMBITION:** To bite a squirrel

Biro of Doom

Dear Mum

Please DON'T hoover our room!

Whatever you do—DON'T HOOVER! And don't let

Piddle in . . .

PLEASE DON'T! It's a matter of life and d

When the pen toppled over it nearly broke Josh in half. The towering post of plastic missed one of his eight legs by a hair, and landed with an immense crash.

Josh shrieked and scuttled away, but the column—which only seconds before he'd been holding easily in his hand—now began to roll, chasing thunderously after him. He

9

shrieked again. He was being chased across an air hockey table by a giant rolling ballpoint.

'Please don't let me get killed by a Biro!' whimpered Josh, cowering against the black wall which edged the air hockey table as the pen skidded towards him like the log of a giant redwood tree. 'Please don't let me— aaaaah!'

Suddenly he was plucked up into the air just as the pen crashed violently into the wall he'd been trapped against. There was a deafening buzzing noise above him and Josh rolled his eight eyes up fearfully.

He had been seized by a flying tank.

'Danny? Danny?' yelled Josh. 'Is that you?'

It was a dark maroon colour—almost black—with antlers. Two huge antlers which were actually its jaws—and it was in these jaws that Josh was now riding. He'd better hope it was Danny. If it wasn't, this creature could squish him at any moment.

On either side of the antler jaws were long feelers with what looked like little hairbrushes on the end of them. Back along the undercarriage he could see six legs and a belly which looked as if it was made of high quality leather.

The rescue aircraft abruptly deposited him on a shiny white strip—the windowsill, he realized—and then landed beside him and shuddered. 'Euuugh!' Its hairbrush feelers quivered. 'I can't believe I just picked up a SPIDER!'

Josh turned to marvel at his twin brother— noticing two wide-set eyes and some fingery mouth parts. 'Now, don't freak, Danny, but . . . WOW! You're a STAG BEETLE!'

Not So Smartie

'I don't care what I am,' moaned Danny. 'I'm freaking OUT! I just picked up a SPIDER!'

'No—you picked up your BROTHER,' corrected Josh. 'Thanks for saving my life!'

Danny wouldn't look at him. He was terrified of spiders and quite a few other creepy-crawlies. The fact that he had been a spider—and a fly, a grasshopper, and an ant—over the past few weeks didn't seem to help his phobia.

'Petty said she would never turn us into creepy-crawlies again!' he muttered angrily. 'She promised! So how did this happen?'

Josh sighed. 'Petty Potts is many things, Danny. She's our neighbour. She's an old lady. She's a genius scientist who can turn us into bugs with her SWITCH spray. She's mad and she thinks government agents are chasing her. What she isn't is TRUSTWORTHY.'

'So—you think she put those Smarties on our air hockey table deliberately?' asked Danny, still avoiding looking at the house spider his brother had recently become. 'She spiked them with SWITCH potion and put them there to see what would happen?'

'That's exactly what I think,' said Josh. 'You ate the orange Smartie and I ate the red Smartie. I was just sitting on the air hockey table reading my book when I saw you disappear and I KNEW she'd done it again! Stag BeetleSWITCH potion must have been in the orange one, and SpiderSWITCH in the other one.'

'But what if we get killed? Swatted? Stamped on? Eaten?' squawked Danny. 'You would've been spider squish under that pen if I hadn't heard you screaming and flown up from the carpet to get you. What about that? Doesn't she care?!'

Josh shrugged. It was a pretty impressive shrug. You can do a lot of shrugging with twenty-four knees. 'She doesn't WANT us to get killed,' he said. 'I think she wants us to go to her lab and get her to switch us back—and then talk to her again. We haven't talked to her for days and she's getting fed up with waiting.'

Danny buzzed up and down the window-pane, head-butting it angrily. 'Well I'm NOT flying anywhere. No WAY. I'm just going to wait here until we turn back into boys again. It shouldn't take long.'

'Hmmmm,' said Josh.

'What?' Danny landed back on the windowsill and stared at Josh, even though his brother's face was terrifying. It was dark brown, with eight eyes stacked up it, and nasty little twiddly fingery bits where its mouth should be. Mandibles, he remembered Josh telling him, the time they'd both been SWITCHed into spiders. Eugh. Nasty.

'Well,' said Josh. 'Two things. One—we don't know how strong the potion in the Smarties was. And I bet it was strong. She knows if we haven't changed back in half an hour we're probably going to give in and go to her for help. And two . . . ' There was a loud clunk that shuddered through the air of their bedroom—once a normal size; now about as big as Wembley Arena. ' . . . it's Mum's hoovering day. She's going to be in here any time now, and if she sees us she'll freak out and suck us to our doom. That's why I wrote the note, begging her not to hoover, as soon as I saw you vanish and realized I was next.'

There was another clunk and a titanic black shadow loomed in the doorway.

'Um—time to go, I think,' squeaked Josh. He didn't fancy a trip up the Hoover nozzle. 'Come on, Danny! Give us a lift! Fast!'

RRRRRRRROOOOOOOOOOOOOO went the Hoover. It was incredibly loud. Danny yelped with horror. He seized Josh around his bulbous brown abdomen, rose up like a helicopter and flew them both out through the gap in the bedroom window.

Beetles in the Hood

It was a warm early summer's evening and
the garden was filled with air traffic. Wasps,
bees, butterflies, dragonflies, gnats, moths
and ladybirds were zooming around like some
kind of mad insect aerial circus.

Danny's wing cases rose high like shiny
ears and from beneath them his wings were
flapping so fast they were making the air
quiver and buzz. Josh had only ever seen
a stag beetle flying twice before—from a
distance—and it was an amazing sight to
see close up. Danny was always calling
his twin brother a 'freaky little bug boffin'
because he was so fascinated by creepy-
crawlies of all kinds.

'Aaaaargh!' Danny suddenly dropped like a sky diver. A particularly large wasp—a hornet, in fact—had just cut across his flight path without any warning.

'What are you DOING?' screamed Josh. The weedy ground was hurtling towards him. 'You're going to break all my LEEEEEGS!'

SNAP! SLOBBER!

'EEEEEEEEEEEEEEEEEEEEK!' screamed both boys. 'PIDDLE!' shouted Josh. Their dog was leaping up towards them from the patio, snapping his pointed white teeth around his lolling pink tongue. He loved to eat creepy-crawlies. For Piddle this was a tasty game of catch!

Danny buzzed twice as loudly as he hauled them both up away from their friendly pet's ravening jaws in a warm blast of dog food scented air. They shot across the top of the fence and then hurtled down into Petty's garden. Josh scrunched his elegant but oh-so-snappable limbs up close to his body and got ready for the crunch. But half a second

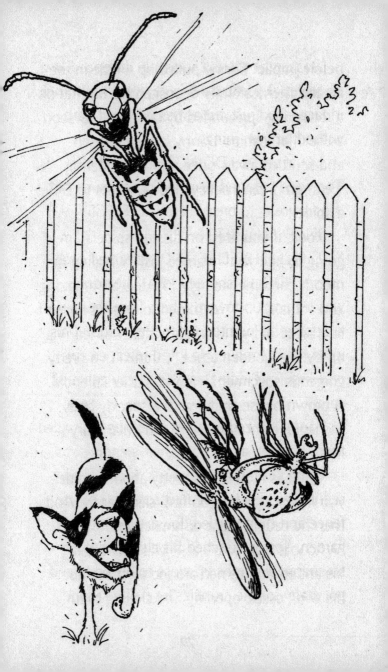

before impact Danny pulled up a little in the air and then carefully deposited his brother on a rotten log surrounded by tall grass. As soon as he'd let Josh go Danny landed himself and scuttled away, once again shuddering. 'Eeuurgh! I can't believe Piddle wants to EAT a spider!'

'Look, if you keep on dissing spiders I'm going to bite you!' warned Josh, wiggling his mouth parts menacingly. 'Spiders are amazing and actually . . .' he turned to inspect himself in a bit of old window glass that was leaning up by the wooden fence, 'I think I'm a pretty gorgeous specimen!' He was rather splendid. A brown house spider with a speckly body, the usual eight eyes, eight muscular hairy legs . . .

'There is NOTHING pretty about a spider, you freaky little bug boffin!' said Danny. And then he caught sight of himself in the glass. 'Whoooa! But look—at—ME!' He raised his antlers and turned around to check out his wing cases, opening and closing them

like twin bonnets on a sleek sports
car, allowing the filmy but tough
wings to shoot out and quiver
with air-readiness. 'I'm a
TRANSFORMER!'

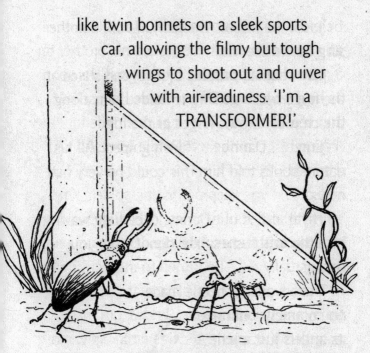

'You are amazing,' agreed Josh. 'And there's
not much which will try to eat you. But me?
I'm a teatime snack just waiting to happen!
Come on—we're already in Petty's garden.
Let's get to the shed and the lab!'

But Danny wasn't paying attention. He
had turned his back on his brother and was
staring down the rotting log at something
incredible. ANOTHER him!

'Josh!' he hissed, excitedly. 'Look! Another stag beetle like me!'

Josh scurried past his brother and stared at the huge beast walking towards them along the crumbly brown ridges of the log.

'Erm . . . Danny . . . ' Josh gulped. All his nature books told him this could be very bad news.

'Hiya!' called out Danny, cheerfully waving his little hairbrushes. 'Helloooo! How you doing?'

The advancing beetle made no comment but raised its antlers just a little higher than Danny's.

'Danneeee . . .' warned Josh. Then he saw
something which made all his legs shake.
The advancing beetle was bad enough . . .
but now coming up on the edge of the log
was something smaller. Same colour but with
daintier jaws. It was a female stag beetle.
The male stag beetle's antlers began to wave
about energetically.

'What's that?? A high five?' Danny was
burbling, unaware of the dreadful danger
he was in, and attempting to slap antlers in
a buddy kind of way. 'Oh—hi!' he added,
spotting the smaller beetle. 'How's tricks?'

Josh jumped on his brother's head. 'STOP! Get away!'

'EEEEEEEUUUGH! GET OFF!' squealed Danny.

Josh fell onto the log between the three beetles in a tangle of terror. Danny ignored him and began cheerfully flapping his little hairbrushes at the small beetle.

'DANNY! That's a GIRL beetle!'

'So?' said Danny, still waving at the girl beetle. 'Hi!'

'And that's her BOYFRIEND!' screeched Josh. 'And he's the JEALOUS TYPE!'

Before he could jump back on Danny's head and get him to fly them both to safety there was a loud CRUNCH and Danny was being spun through the air.

He landed on his back with a crack and slid a little way along the log as the stag beetle advanced on him. He was waving back, but he wasn't saying 'Hi . . .'

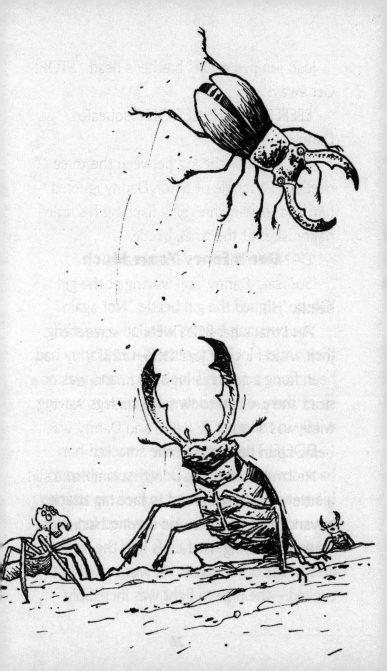

Don't Fancy Yours Much

'Oh no,' sighed the girl beetle. 'Not again.'

The two stag beetles were now wrestling, their antlers locked together—but Danny had been flung across his foe's back, and was now stuck there, upside down, his six legs waving wildly in the air.

DOOF! The bigger beetle smacked him back down on the log. Danny scrambled to his feet and turned round to face his attacker, antlers going up again. He rammed forwards, driving the two spiked ends into the throat area of the other beetle. He was scared but excited—the urge to fight was incredibly strong. He felt like a gladiator.

The bigger beetle thwacked his antlers down on Danny's head and they both turned round and round, pushing and shoving and grunting, neither one giving up the fight.

'Danny! Come away!' shrieked Josh, wringing his palps with anxiety. He knew stag beetle battles could go on for ages and often ended in death.

'Don't, Rick!' shouted the girl beetle, just behind him. 'It's not worth it!'

Josh squirmed in underneath the circling beetles, like a mechanic under two runaway trucks. He poked his face up in front of Danny's, which was straining and grimacing in the midst of the battle. 'What are you doing?' he demanded. 'Why are you fighting?!'

'Grrrrrrrr!' commented Danny.

'OK—let me get this straight!' hissed Josh, scampering backwards as the bigger beetle's shoving got more successful. 'You want a girlfriend?'

29

'What?!' snapped Danny, shoving back as hard as he could, with a long fierce gurgle.

'You want to go out . . . with a beetle?' Josh waved his palps at his brother in a questioning way. 'You want to take old forklift chops over there out for a movie and milkshakes and smoochies?'

'WHAT ARE YOU *ON* ABOUT? YEEEEAAAARRGH . . . ' Danny was once again spun up through the air and thrown onto his opponent's back.

Josh sighed and then jumped up to join him. The big beetle didn't seem to have noticed him at all. 'You're FIGHTING over a GIRL, you dingbat!' he yelled.

'What . . . her?' Danny struggled up through the antler-grip and twisted back upright to stare at the smaller beetle who was watching the fight with a rather bored expression. 'I don't even FANCY her!'

Suddenly he was back on the log, spinning on his wing case with his legs in the air again. A shadow fell across him as his opponent growled down at him. 'Oi! Are you sayin' my girlfriend's ugly?'

'No! No!' squeaked Danny. 'She's . . . ' He glanced at the female beetle who was raising one of her little hairbrush feelers at him like an eyebrow, waiting. 'She's beautiful . . . ' went on Danny. He struggled back to his feet and began to back away. 'And I am not worthy of her . . . '

The male beetle stared at Danny, antlers held high, but did not advance again.

'Honestly . . . she's a babe . . . ' muttered Danny, edging away backwards as Josh ran alongside him. 'And perfect for you . . . I mean . . . check out those . . . lovely . . . er . . . feelers . . . '

'Time to go,' said Josh.

Danny didn't need telling twice. He grabbed his brother and took to the sky.

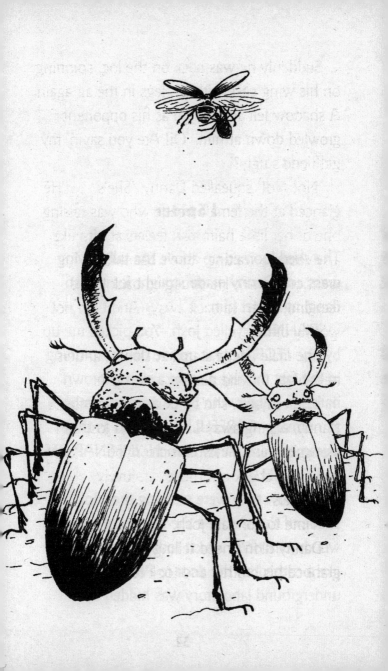

I Spider

The shed loomed up above the tall waving grass and Danny made straight for it, Josh dangling under him.

'DANNEE!' yelled Josh. 'You picked me up by one LEG!' He was upside down, spinning in the fast moving air, like a skinny brown ballerina (albeit with twice as many limbs as normal). 'CAREFUL!' he yelped as they skimmed past a leafy branch. 'It'll SNAP OFF and I'll FALL!'

But now they were entering the cool shade of the shed. At the far end of the woody chamber, which today seemed like a cathedral, the door to Petty's secret underground laboratory was hidden by a curtain of old sacking. Danny had to land. He dumped Josh at the foot of the sacking and landed next to him, panting.

'Josh,' he said, after he'd got his breath back. Josh was counting his legs. He was amazed to find he still had all eight, 'Josh . . . I like wrestling!'

'Yes,' muttered Josh. 'You're a stag beetle. You're programmed to like it. All you want to do is fight off other stag beetles and get yourself a girlfriend. If you'd spent about three years grubbing about underground and you suddenly got wings, trust me, you'd want to live it LARGE. Fly about, have punch ups, chase the girls . . . '

'This is the coolest thing I've been yet!' said Danny.

'Yeah . . . just until you fall down dead in about two weeks' time,' said Josh.

'What? Nooo! I'm big and strong!'

'Stag beetles don't even eat,' said Josh. 'They only last for a couple of months of fighting and beetle smoochies . . . and then they die.'

'So . . . cruel . . . ' Danny sighed.

'It's worse for me,' muttered Josh. 'If I ever get a girlfriend there's a good chance she'll eat me.'

They looked at each other. 'PETTEEEEEE!' they yelled.

It was time to find the only human who could get them out of this mess. The one who'd put them in it.

BEEP! BEEP! BEEP!

The high-pitched sound rang through the air—along with a hollow crash behind the sacking.

Beep! Beep! Beep!

'She's coming!' shouted Danny. 'LOOK OUT!' And then they were both swept up on a tidal wave of sacking material which flung them into the shadowy cave of a fallen wellington boot.

It smelt rubbery and mildewy and worse, lived in. A steely network of silk strands clung to one side of the welly cave. Suddenly, out of nowhere, a very big black spider came running for them.

'Aaaaaaaargh!' yelled Josh. There was no escape—this beast was way bigger and stronger than he was—a garden shed spider. A trapdoor type. Fast and deadly. They must have hit one of its tripwires and alerted it to their presence.

Then, to his amazement, a big red antler came crashing down on the many-eyed face of the black spider, knocking it unconscious.

'Whoooa! Danny! That was SO cool!' marvelled Josh as they legged it back out of the welly. 'You saved me—a spider—from a spider!'

The beeping got suddenly VERY LOUD and three seconds later they were both sliding around a plastic tub.

'Phew!' said Danny. 'About TIME!'

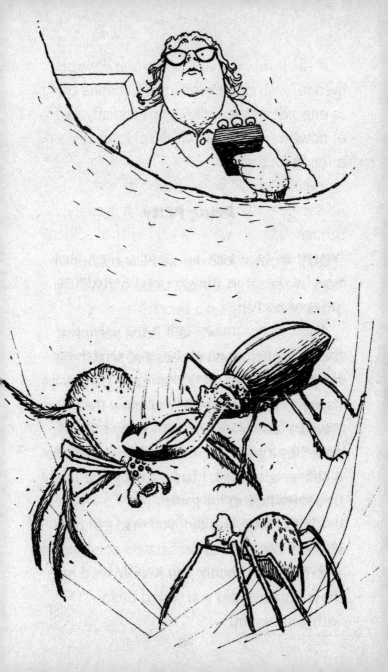

Being Petty

'YOU!' shouted Josh. He and Danny, human boys again, sat in a misty cloud of SWITCH antidote on Petty's lab bench.

'Er . . . yes . . . me,' said Petty, peering at them over her round glasses and scratching her grey hair. 'But don't thank me. I'm always happy to save your lives, you know that.' She waved a little black box with shiny buttons on it. 'It's a good job my SWITCHee Detector is still working well. I had a feeling you might be somewhere in my garden.'

'Of COURSE you did, you mad granny!' shrieked Danny. 'You deliberately poisoned us with SWITCH potion. You KNEW we'd eat those Smarties and you spiked them with your serum!'

Petty smiled at him. 'Well how else was
I to get you to come and see me? Josh!
Danny! You know I'm depending on you
to help me find the missing cubes with the
code for REPTOSWITCH! And you haven't
bothered looking for weeks, have you? And
you're never in when I call. Without your
help my Serum Which Instigates Total
Cellular Hijack will never move on to reptile
level!'

Danny and Josh looked at each other, shaking their heads. Petty Potts was shameless. She did not CARE how much danger she put them in. And this was exactly why they had decided to stay away from her for a while (even though they had still kept a look out for her last two missing REPTOSWITCH cubes).

'Look—I know you're cross with me and I'm sorry.' She grinned, looking about as sorry as a puppy with a new squeaky toy.

'But you have to know . . . everything we have worked for . . . all the hours spent searching for the secret formula . . . the

REPTOSWITCH cubes you've already found for me. It's all going to pay off . . . soon. Just find me the last two cubes and you'll find out what it's like to be . . . '

Danny narrowed his eyes at her. 'A snake . . . ?'

'An alligator?' added Josh.

'YES!' Petty punched the air and stared towards the wobbly metal roof of the secret lab with a wild light in her eyes. 'Once I have PERFECTED REPTOSWITCH! One day . . . very soon . . . you will both test it out.'

'Daneeeee . . . Jo-osh . . . Teatime . . . '
Their mum's voice wafted down from the
normal world as Danny and Josh tried to think
of what to say next.

'No,' said Danny, at last. 'Your SWITCH
sprays are just TOO dangerous.'

Josh nodded. 'And you don't CARE what
they do to us.'

Petty looked hurt. 'I do! I do! I just saved
your lives didn't I?'

'DANEEEEE . . . JO-OSH . . . COME IN
NOW . . . '

'Don't you want to be a snake? A lizard? A
DRAGON?!!' Petty looked bewildered.

'There's no such thing as dragons,' said
Danny.

'Let's go home to tea,' said Josh
and he and Danny left.

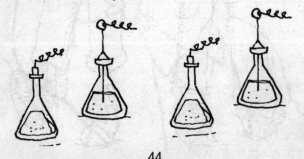

44

Petty stared after them for a few seconds and then her face creased into a smile.

'They'll be back,' she said, to nobody in particular. 'YESSS! They'll be BACK! And when they do come back . . . when they DO . . . Bwah-haha-haha-ha—'

'Oh, hang on,' said Josh, stepping back into the lab. 'Dropped 10p.' He collected the coin off the bench and nodded at Petty as she paused in mid evil cackle. 'Bye.'

'—haha-haha-haha!' she finished.

She sniffed.

She went to have a cup of Ovaltine.

S.W.I.T.C.H.
SERUM WHICH INSTIGATES TOTAL CELLULAR HIJACK

Whether you're interested in insects or terrified of tarantulas, you'll love the S.W.I.T.C.H. website!

Find out more about the creatures in Josh and Danny's adventures, enter fantastic competitions, read the first chapters of all of the S.W.I.T.C.H. books, and enjoy creepy-crawly games and activities.

www.switch-books.co.uk

Other books

in the S.W.I.T.C.H. series

If you enjoyed **Gargoylz Make Some Noise**, you might like to try some of these other adventures!

Gargoylz on the Loose!

Gargoylz Get Up to Mischief

Gargoylz at a Midnight Feast

Gargoylz Take a Trip

Gargoylz Put on a Show

Gargoylz Have Fun at the Fair

Gargoylz Go to a Party

Gargoylz: Magic at the Museum

Gargoylz Make a Splash!

Gargoylz Ride to the Rescue

Gargoylz Make a Movie

Gargoylz Summer Fun

Gargoylz on the Go!

Gargoylz Save Christmas

Visit **www.gargoylz.co.uk** for fun weekly blogs, cool games, competitions and much more!

Gargoylz

Make Some Noise

Gargoylz: grotesque stone creatures found on old buildings, spouting rainwater from the guttering. Sometimes seen causing mischief and mayhem before scampering away over rooftops.

Meet the Gargoylz!

Full name: Tobias the Third

Known as: Toby

Special Power: Flying

Likes: All kinds of pranks and mischief – especially playing jokes on the vicar

Dislikes: Mrs Hogsbottom, garden gnomes

Name: Cyrus

Special Power: Singing lullabies to send humanz to sleep

Likes: Fun dayz out

Dislikes: Snoring

Full name: Zackary

Known as: Zack

Special Power: Making himself invisible to humanz

Likes: Bouncing around, eating bramblz, thistlz, and anything with pricklz!

Dislikes: Keeping still

Full name: Theophilus

Known as: Theo

Special Power: Turning into a ferocious tiger (well, tabby kitten!)

Likes: Sunny spots and cosy places

Dislikes: Rain

Full name: Enoch

Special Power: Doing the voices of any character he's ever read about

Likes: Exciting stories and learning new pranks

Dislikes: Loud, scary noises

Full name: Jehieli

Known as: Jelly

Special Power: Turning to jelly

Likes: Having friendz to play with

Dislikes: Bulliez and spoilsports

GARGOYLZ MAKE SOME NOISE
A RED FOX BOOK 978 0 956 62761 2

First published in Great Britain by Red Fox,
an imprint of Random House Children's Books
A Random House Group Company

This edition published specially for World Book Day 2011

1 3 5 7 9 10 8 6 4 2

Series created and developed by Amber Caravéo
Copyright © Random House Children's Books, 2011

Set in Bembo Schoolbook

Red Fox Books are published by Random House Children's Books,
61–63 Uxbridge Road, London W5 5SA

www.**kids**at**randomhouse**.co.uk
www.**rbooks**.co.uk

Addresses for companies within The Random House Group Limited can be
found at: www.randomhouse.co.uk/offices.htm

THE RANDOM HOUSE GROUP Limited Reg. No. 954009

A CIP catalogue record for this book is available from the British Library.

This book has been specially written and published for World Book Day 2011.
World Book Day is a worldwide celebration of books and reading,
with events held last year in countries part as far apart as
Afghanistan and Australia, Nigeria and Uruguay.
For Further information please see www.**worldbookday**.com
World Book Day in the UK and Ireland is made possible by generous
sponsorship from National Book Tokens, participating publishers, authors
and booksellers. Booksellers who accept the £1 World Book Day Token
kindly agree to bear the full cost of redeeming it.

Printed and bound in Great Britain by Cox and Wyman

Qargoylz

Make Some Noise

Burchett & Vogler

illustrated by Leighton Noyes

RED FOX

For our editor, Ruth Knowles, who looks after the Gargoylz so well.
- **Burchett & Vogler**

For my beautiful daughter Elodie – I close my eyes and dream of days to come, Daddy xx
- **Leighton Noyes**

1. Fairy Trouble

"All aboard the jet-bus!" yelled Max Black.

"We're on the biggest superspy mission
of all time!" his best friend, Ben Neal, called
back.

They scrambled onto the coach that was
waiting outside Oldacre Primary School.
Year Four were off to the central library
in the nearby town, where two famous
authors were going to tell them all about
their books. It was up to the pupils to decide
which one they wanted to see.

"Troy Brawn's the best!" exclaimed Max.
"I can't wait to meet him."

"His *Spy-boy* books are the most

1

awesome stories in the history of most awesome stories," agreed Ben.

"I'm glad we're not going to be stuck listening to Lily Twinkletoes," said Max in disgust as they threw themselves into the back seats. "She writes all about stupid fairies!"

Lucinda Tellingly spun round and glared at them. "Fairies aren't stupid," she snapped.

"Her *Princess Castle* books are lovely. They're full of magic and palaces and glittery things."

"Sounds yucky to me," said Ben.

Max nodded. "Double yucky!"

Lucinda sniffed and turned back to her friends.

The moment they arrived at the library, Max and Ben were off the coach and bursting through the big swing doors.

The librarian scurried along to meet them all, looking worried. She went straight up to their teacher and whispered something in her ear.

Miss Bleet immediately flapped her hands and called for silence. "I'm sorry, but one of our authors can't be with us today," she announced.

"Don't let it be Troy Brawn," whispered Ben, crossing his fingers. "Don't let it be Troy Brawn."

"It's Troy Brawn," Miss Bleet went on. "His car won't start."

Max and Ben turned to each other in horror.

"That's terrible," groaned Max. "Hasn't he got a spy-mobile?"

"Or jet-propelled spy-boots?" suggested Ben desperately.

"Or a spy-rocket like in *Spy-boy Saves Saturn*?" added Max. "That would get him here in minutes!"

"In seconds!" cried Ben.

"I can see you're great Troy Brawn fans!" said the librarian with a smile. "But don't worry, we've got an author here that you'll have just as much fun with – Lily Twinkletoes!"

She tripped off towards a huge hall

decorated in twinkling lights.

Max looked horrified. "I'm going to be sick."

"Me too," said Ben, holding his tummy. "A whole hour of glitter and frills. We won't survive!"

"No boys in the whole world should have to put up with that," said Max.

"No boys in the whole *universe*," corrected Ben.

Miss Bleet ushered everyone towards the hall, where two smiling helpers with shiny wings on their backs were waiting. Before Max realized what was happening, the fairy assistants popped a tiara on his head and pressed a fluffy pink wand into his hand.

Ben burst out laughing, but he soon stopped when he found himself with a silver crown in his spiky hair and a glittery stick in his fist.

There was a blinding flash of light, and stars danced in front of the boys' eyes.

"I've just taken a photo of you two for the local paper!" chirped the librarian, waving a camera at them. "You'll be pleased to know you'll be on the front page of the *Oldacre Gazette* next week." And she trotted off to adjust the loudspeakers at the front of the hall.

The boys stared after her with open mouths.

"That's terrible!" gasped Ben. "Everyone in the village will see us dressed as fairies!"

"We'll have to stay in our houses for ever!" cried Max.

"Or go out with paper bags over our heads," added Ben gloomily.

He felt something poke him in the elbow. It was Lucinda's wand. "You're blocking the way," she said crossly. "Hurry up and get in the hall. We don't want to miss a moment of the talk."

She rushed off to get seats in the front row, giggling excitedly with her friends. Max and Ben mooched over and sat at the very back.

They were about to rip off their tiaras when they saw the librarian looking their way.

"Secret Plan: Delete That Photo!" muttered Max, grinning weakly and waving his wand at her.

"But how can we get hold of the camera?" asked Ben. "The librarian's going to sit right at the front. She's miles away from us."

"I'll crawl under the chairs," said Max. "Like Spy-boy in *Spy-boy and the Theatre of Death*."

He was just diving under the chair in front when Miss Bleet plonked herself into it. She peered down at Max in surprise. "Whatever are you doing?" she asked him.

He hurriedly scrambled up. "Just making sure your seat is fairyproof, miss."

"Bad luck, Agent Black!" hissed Ben as Max took his seat again.

"It's all right, Agent Neal, I've got a new plan," replied Max. "We get up on the roof, lower ourselves with a fishing rod and—"

All of a sudden a shower of sparkles fluttered down over the stage and tinkling music wafted from the speakers. A plump lady in a pink tutu and wings skipped out and gave a curtsey.

"Hello, children," she trilled. "I'm Lily Twinkletoes. Are you ready for a super-sweet fairy adventure?"

"Yes!" came an excited chorus from the girls.

"No!" groaned Max and Ben, slumping lower in their seats.

But as the music died away, they heard gruff, growly chuckles coming from somewhere in the room.

Max sat bolt upright. "Our troubles are over," he said in Ben's ear. "Our gargoyle friends are here!"

The gargoylz were ugly stone statues that hung on the ancient church next door to Oldacre Primary School. The boys had been delighted when they discovered that the little creatures could come to life, and liked nothing better than to play tricks with them.

"Awesome!" replied Ben. "But where are they?"

The boys looked eagerly about the hall, scanning the walls, the ceiling and the balcony that ran around the sides.

"There — on that window ledge!" hissed Ben as four grinning faces peeped out from behind a curtain. It's Cyrus and Jelly . . ."

". . . and Toby and Theo!" added Max. "Brilliant! They'll be able to help us get the camera."

Pop! A grinning gargoyle appeared under Miss Bleet's seat. Max activated his spy radar: lion's mane, stony skin, cheeky gleam in his eyes. He knew what that meant. It was Zack. Every gargoyle had a special power, and Zack could make himself invisible.

"Tinsel and tiaraz," Zack burst out, pointing at the boys in their fairy decorations and laughing. "Tinsel and tiaraz!"

Miss Bleet swung round to glare at Max and Ben. Zack popped out of sight just in time.

"Sorry, miss," called Ben. "I didn't mean to shout out *Tinsel and tiaras*. I just got overexcited. Lily Twinkletoes is such fun." He wriggled in his seat and flapped his hands

about. "*Tinsel and tiaras*," he chanted feebly.

Miss Bleet beamed at him. "I knew you boys would like the fairies."

As she turned back to join in a song about waving wands and fluttering feathers, Zack reappeared, chuckling.

"You've arrived in the nick of time," whispered Max. "We need help." He quickly told Zack about the ghastly photo and their secret plan to delete it. "And I know the very gargoyle who can help us get that camera," he finished. "Cyrus!"

"You're right," said Ben. "Cyrus can use his special power to sing everyone to sleep. Then it'll be easy-peasy to run up and delete the photo."

"I'll go and tell him," announced Zack. "Gargoylz to the rescue!" **Pop!** He vanished. Then – **pop!** – he reappeared for a second. "Don't forget to cover your earz, boyz."

In a flash, the boys had their fingers in their ears to stop themselves falling asleep too.

And just in time – Cyrus was already
stepping out onto
the window ledge.
The gargoyle flung
out his arms and
opened his mouth,
to reveal rows of
sharp teeth. All
around the two
boys, children and

teachers closed their eyes and slumped in
their seats as a beautiful lullaby filled the
hall. As soon as Max saw Cyrus stop singing,
he grabbed Ben's arm. "Time for our secret
plan."

They dashed up to the librarian, who
was fast asleep, with her head flung back.
Max tried to ease the camera out of her
grasp but she grunted and gripped it more
tightly.

"It's no use," he hissed. "I can't shift it."

"We need to get out of here," said Ben.
"Then we can make a new secret plan

with the gargoylz."

They sprinted out into the corridor, threw down their wands and tore off their tiaras. The place was empty except for a security man, who was snoring loudly with his head on his desk.

Toby, Theo, Cyrus and Jelly burst out from behind a leaflet stand and scampered over to the boys. Then – **pop!** – Zack appeared in the middle of them.

Cyrus tapped Max on the leg. "My singing was brilliant!" he exclaimed, grinning broadly and showing rows of pointy teeth. "That should keep them quiet for a day or two."

"Ten minutes if we're lucky," whispered Toby, swooping down to land on Ben's shoulder, a wide grin on his monkey face.

"Cyrus's power doesn't last as long as he thinks."

"Well, at least it got us out of there," said Max. "Thanks, Cyrus. We may not have got the photo yet but I was beginning to feel my brain turn sparkly."

Jelly nodded his pterodactyl beak. "I'm awfully glad we decided to hide in the school bus and come with you," he said earnestly. "Watching the humanz fall asleep was jolly funny!"

"But not as funny as seeing Max and Ben in pink glittery things," said Toby, his golden eyes brimming with mischief. "I haven't laughed so much since Cyrus hid in the vicar's fruit bowl and pelted him with bananas."

"We didn't ask to wear that fairy stuff," said Ben. "We were hoping to hear all about secret agents." He told the gargoylz about

Troy Brawn and his car.

"You don't need a silly author," said Theo, waving his stripy tail. "You've got us to have fun with."

"Don't know why you're bothering with silly old books anyway," added Cyrus. "Let's play some more tricks!"

"Good idea," said Ben. "As long as it gets us that camera."

At that moment the security man snorted, lifted his head and stared at his desk, puzzled. He gave a huge yawn and began to stretch.

"Hide!" said Max urgently. "Everyone's waking up!"

"Through there!" Ben spotted a scruffy old door behind them and pushed it open.

They all tried to rush through it at once and fell down in a tangle of arms and legs and wings. At last they were inside and Toby slammed the door shut. The room was plunged into darkness.

Suddenly they heard the security man's footsteps plodding towards the door. "Who's there?" came his gruff voice.

"Shouldn't we answer?" hissed Jelly. "It would be polite."

"No we shouldn't," Max hissed back.

At last the man shuffled away down the corridor.

"We're safe!" whispered Ben when it had all gone quiet. "But where are we?"

Max fumbled about the wall trying to find a light switch. "I can feel books," he said, running his hand over the spines. "Hundreds of them. Thousands! And they're really dusty."

WAAA-TISH-OOOOOO!

An almighty sneeze exploded above their heads.

"Who was that?" came Theo's voice.

"Was that you, Max?"

"Not me," said Max.

"Nor me," said Ben.

"Nor us," cried all the gargoylz together.

"Then who was it?" quavered Toby.

2. Whoooo's There?

Max and Ben felt stony paws gripping their legs as the gargoylz clung to them in terror.

"It's a ghost!" squealed Zack.

"A ghastly ghost!" shrieked Jelly.

"A ghastly ghost with a ghastly cold," wailed Cyrus.

At that moment Max found the light switch and flicked it on. Now they could see that they were in a storeroom lined with shelves and shelves of dusty books.

"Where's the ghost?" growled Theo. "I'll turn into a fierce tiger and protect you. My roar will terrify him, and then I'll gobble him up. Bold tigerz like me can

19

gobble ghosts up no problem."

Theo thought he turned into a fierce tiger, but as he was still a young gargoyle – just four hundred and twelve years old – he could only manage to become a cute kitten.

"Oooooh!" came a wail from the top shelf.

Theo leaped in terror, bounced off a pile of books, cannoned into Cyrus and fell on top of Toby.

The voice came again: "Please don't gobble me up. I'm not a ghost and I haven't done anything wrong."

Max and Ben peered at the top shelf. At first they could only see a row of thick encyclopaedias. But then they noticed that one of the heavy books was open. Two huge round eyes were blinking at them from over the spine.

"Who are you?" asked Ben in amazement.

The book slowly closed and a strange creature shuffled out of the darkness. It was covered in stony feathers, with tufts for ears and dark marks around its eyes as if it was wearing glasses. It looked like a wise old owl.

"Whooo am I?" it said. "I'm Enoch – I'm a gargoyle."

The gargoylz gave excited cheers.

"Just like us!" called Jelly.

"Spluttering gutterz!" exclaimed Toby, flying up to perch on the top shelf. "Pleased to meet you, Enoch. I'm Toby." He held out a wing and the new gargoyle solemnly shook it with a claw. "Me and my friendz live on Saint Mark's Church in Oldacre."

Enoch swivelled his head to peer down at the other gargoylz, who were grinning and waving to him. Then he spotted the boys.

"But yooou are not gargoylz," he said, his eyes growing even wider. "Whooo are yooou?"

"We're Max and Ben," Max began to explain. "We're boys and we're really pleased—"

The new gargoyle slapped his wings over his head and began to tremble.

"Hooomanz!" came his muffled voice. "Gargoylz mustn't be seen by hooomanz.

Here I am, minding my own business in the peace and quiet with my books, and now hooomanz come along. Boooo-hoooo!"

Cyrus scrambled up the shelves to join him. "Don't worry," he said. "Max and Ben are special humanz. They're our friendz."

Enoch stopped trembling and lowered his wings again. "That's a relief!" he said. "Then you're all welcome to stay – but dooo try to keep quiet." He hopped down a couple of shelves. "I've only been in the library twooo hundred years and I've still got so many books to read."

"Haven't you got any chumz in here?" asked Jelly.

"Books are my chumz," replied Enoch. "And I don't really like being disturbed when I'm reading. Yooou only found out I was here because I sneezed."

"But you're a gargoyle," exclaimed Theo in surprise. "Don't you want to play tricks and pranks? They're much more fun than dusty old books."

"You could play tricks on the people who come in here," suggested Toby.

"Not many people come in this roooom," said Enoch. "And when they dooo, I hide till they've gone. Tricks don't sound like fun."

The gargoylz looked at each other in utter shock.

"A gargoyle who doesn't play tricks!" exclaimed Jelly. "How frightful!"

"Terrible," agreed Zack.

"Tricks are great," Ben told Enoch. "Jumping out to scare someone, or putting chewing gum on your teacher's chair, or . . ."

". . . or distracting everybody so that we can get the librarian's camera," finished Max firmly.  "Remember, we've still got to delete that photo before Lily Twinkletoes has finished her silly talk."

"Good point!" Ben told Enoch about the photo that was going to appear in the paper. "If only we had a super-strong magnet," he sighed. "We could hide in the doorway, pull the camera out of the hall, delete the picture and sneak it back."

Enoch nodded wisely. "Ah yes, you're thinking of how Spy-boy defeated the Ironbots in *Spy-boy and the Mega Magnet*."

Max and Ben gawped at the owly gargoyle.

"Do you know Troy Brawn's books?" asked Max in amazement.

"I read all the children's books as soooon as they come in," said Enoch. "There were one million and seven last time I counted, but Troy Brawn's are my favourites." Suddenly his voice changed completely and he sounded like a young man, brave and daring. "*Never fear, Spy-boy's here,*" he chanted.

"Awesome!" gasped Ben. "Spy-boy's catchphrase. And that's just how I imagined he would speak."

"You were whizzo!" declared Jelly. "I thought someone else had come in."

"Someone invisible like me!" Zack agreed.

"Can you do other voicez?" asked Cyrus.

"Of course," said Enoch. "It's my special power."

"That is so cool!" said Ben.

"Do the Slippery Shadow from *Spy-boy in Deadly Danger,*" Max urged him. "He's one of the creepiest villains ever."

Enoch opened his beak, and out came a sly, sneaky voice that sent shivers down the boys' backs. "*So, Spy-boy! You think you can*

escape from my evil egg-beating machine?"

"That was fantastic!" yelled Ben.

"You're tooo kind," said Enoch shyly. He hunched his shoulders and stood on one leg.  "*Say goodbye to your superspy kit, Spy-boy,*" he rasped. "*You'll never find it once I've thrown it off this high cliff.*"

"And that was the Terrible Tangoman from *Spy-boy Hits the Heights,*" said Ben.

Max punched the air. "That's given me an awesome idea. Spy-boy uses a bungee rope to dive off the cliff and get his superspy kit back. We could sneak up to the balcony, drop down on the librarian and whisk the camera away."

"Brilliant," cried Ben. "Except for one small problem: we don't have a bungee rope."

Everyone scratched their heads and thought.

"We've got Jelly!" Max realized at last. "When he uses his special power he's *very* stretchy."

"Delighted to help!" said Jelly eagerly.

The next instant he'd melted into a blob of purple goo that giggled loudly as Max rolled it into a long tube, thin as wire. They all looked at it admiringly.

"Jelly's so thin no one will even notice him!" exclaimed Cyrus.

"Let's go," said Toby.

"There's another small problem," Ben pointed out. "We don't have Spy-boy to drop down on the librarian."

"Never fear, Zack-boy's here!" yelled Zack, bouncing up and down in excitement. "I'll do it. No one will see me."

"Just what we need!" said Max. "We'll tie one end of Jelly-the-bungee-rope around your waist, Zack. Then, when you bounce down and get the camera, we delete the photo, you replace the camera and – hey presto! – secret plan success!"

"Dangling drainpipes!" declared Toby. "What a trick. No one will believe it when they see a flying camera!"

"But they mustn't," said Max, looking worried. "I hadn't thought of that. We need a diversion."

"I've thought of something that would be perfect," said Ben. "If Enoch does some of

his voices in the hall, the audience will enjoy them so much they'll never notice us taking the camera."

Everyone turned to look at Enoch. The little gargoyle shuffled his feet and blinked in embarrassment. "I–I'm not t-toooo sure I can dooo that," he stammered.

"Of course you can," Toby insisted. "You'll be fantastic."

"It'll be your first gargoyle trick," said Theo.

"And you'd be helping Max and Ben," added Zack.

"If yooou put it like that," said Enoch, fluttering his wings nervously, "I really can't say no."

The gargoylz cheered in delight and Enoch went bright red.

Ben pushed open the stiff door and peered out.

The security man was no longer at his desk. "Coast's clear," he whispered.

Carefully carrying Jelly-the-bungee-rope, Max tiptoed out along the corridor, Ben and the gargoylz behind him. But when they got to the stairs that led to the balcony, Enoch was nowhere to be seen.

Max looked back to see a stony beak poking nervously round the door of the storeroom.

"I don't usually come out of here until the library's closed for the evening," Enoch whispered in fright.

Cyrus scuttled over and took him by a wing. "We'll look after you," he said.

Enoch gulped and waddled out. Holding tightly onto Cyrus, he followed the gargoylz up the stairs. When they reached the balcony, they peered over the rail. Lily Twinkletoes was clodhopping all over the stage, waving her wand. Everyone was watching her – even the security man, who was now sitting at the back, a tiara

31

perched on his peaked cap.

"She's going on about princess dresses," whispered Ben. "Yuck!"

"*I can see the camera!*" squealed Zack. "*I can see the camera.*" He wriggled with excitement and nearly tumbled over the edge.

"It's on the librarian's lap," said Max. "You're going to have to be as cunning as Spy-boy was in *Spy-boy Outsneaks Sneakman.*"

He tied Jelly-the-bungee-rope around Zack's middle.

"Ready to do your voices, Enoch?" asked Toby.

Enoch shuffled along the balcony until he was on the opposite side of the hall. They could just see his huge eyes blinking in the gloom. Max gave him a thumbs-up sign.

A booming pirate voice rang out: "*Aye, aye, mates! Fifteen men on a dead man's chest.*"

"That's Long John Silver from *Treasure Island*!" whispered Ben.

Lily Twinkletoes stopped in the middle of a merry song about sequins and looked puzzled.

"*In the name of King Richard the Lionheart, I will fight you, you evil Sheriff of Nottingham.*" The bold voice thundered all over the hall.

"And that's Robin Hood," exclaimed Max. "Awesome."

There was a stir as the audience gazed about in surprise. Enoch's voices echoed around the walls.

"That's not part of my talk!" called Lily Twinkletoes. "What's going on?"

"Is the library haunted?" quavered Miss Bleet, turning pale.

At this, Lucinda and her friends clutched each other in terror.

"*Fee, fi, fo, fum!*" thundered Enoch.

Lucinda let out a shriek. "It's the books in the library. They're coming to life. They're out to get us. Help!"

She dived under her chair.

"This is brilliant!" whispered Ben. "The trick's working even better than we thought."

"Don't worry, everyone," the librarian was saying cheerfully. "It's probably just the sound system gone funny. I expect we're picking up the radio or something."

She scampered over to one of the speakers, pressed her ear to it and listened intently.

"She's left her camera on her seat," hissed Max. "Ready, Zack?"

Zack jumped off the balcony rail, did a triple somersault and dived down into the hall, popping invisible as he went.

Jelly-the-bungee-rope unwound in a flash.
Max held the other end tightly. The rope
jerked and – **pop!** – Zack bounced back,
clutching the camera in his stony paws.

Ben turned on the camera and reeled back in horror. A picture of him and Max, glittering brightly with tiaras and wands, filled the screen. The gargoylz chuckled merrily.

"Now to get rid of those ghastly faces — as Spy-boy said when he fought the ten-headed Snakeman." As the mystery voices continued to fill the air, Ben quickly deleted the photo and handed the camera to Zack. "You know what to do, Zack-boy."

The excited little gargoyle leaped off on Jelly-the-bungee-rope and disappeared again. Max peered over and watched the

camera plummeting towards its destination. Luckily everyone below was too busy clutching each other and wailing to notice. But at that moment the librarian turned back from the speakers and saw her camera flying through the air.

"Aaaargh!" she screamed. "The library *is* haunted! Let me out!"

Pop! Zack splatted into the wall behind the boys and slid down in a heap.

"Fairy Photo Mission Success!" he exclaimed, shaking his mane. "Took an extra snap on the way down!"

"Good trick, Zack!" whispered Max. "The librarian will think the library ghost took it! And awesome work, Jelly."

Jelly-the-bungee-rope coiled into a ball and turned back into the grinning little pterodactyl.

"That was a jolly jape," he said. "There's nothing like a nice stretch!"

Enoch came waddling along the balcony. "Were my voices any gooood?" he asked shyly. "I'm not sure the audience liked them."

"You were a star!" exclaimed Ben. "We wouldn't have been able to do the trick without you."

Enoch grinned broadly.

"I haven't had so much fun since Zack pinched the vicar's remote control and made him watch seven episodes of *Pixie Playtime*," said Toby. "Libraries aren't so bad after all. And some books even sound exciting!"

"And I think tricks are lots of fun," admitted Enoch. "In fact I'd say they're a hooooot!"

There was a sudden cheer from the hall below.

"Hi, kids!" came a deep voice. "Who wants to hear about Spy-boy?"

Max peeped over the balcony and turned

to the others, his eyes wide with delight. "Troy Brawn's here!" he gasped. "He's made it."

"We've got to get down there and meet him, Agent Black!" cried Ben.

"Too right, Agent Neal," replied Max. "But how are we going to get back into the hall without being seen?"

"My turn to help," said Theo, tapping him with a paw. "I'll dash down onto the stage and turn into a tiger. Everyone will be so terrified they won't notice you coming in!"

"Brilliant," said Ben. He winked at Max. "They won't be able to take their eyes off you, Theo."

"And then I'm going to take the gargoylz on a tour of the library," said Enoch. "They can teach me some more tricks."

"Have fun, gargoylz!" called Max as the boys followed Theo to the stairs.

"We will," chorused their stony friends.